ISLAMABAD
TILFORD, SURREY

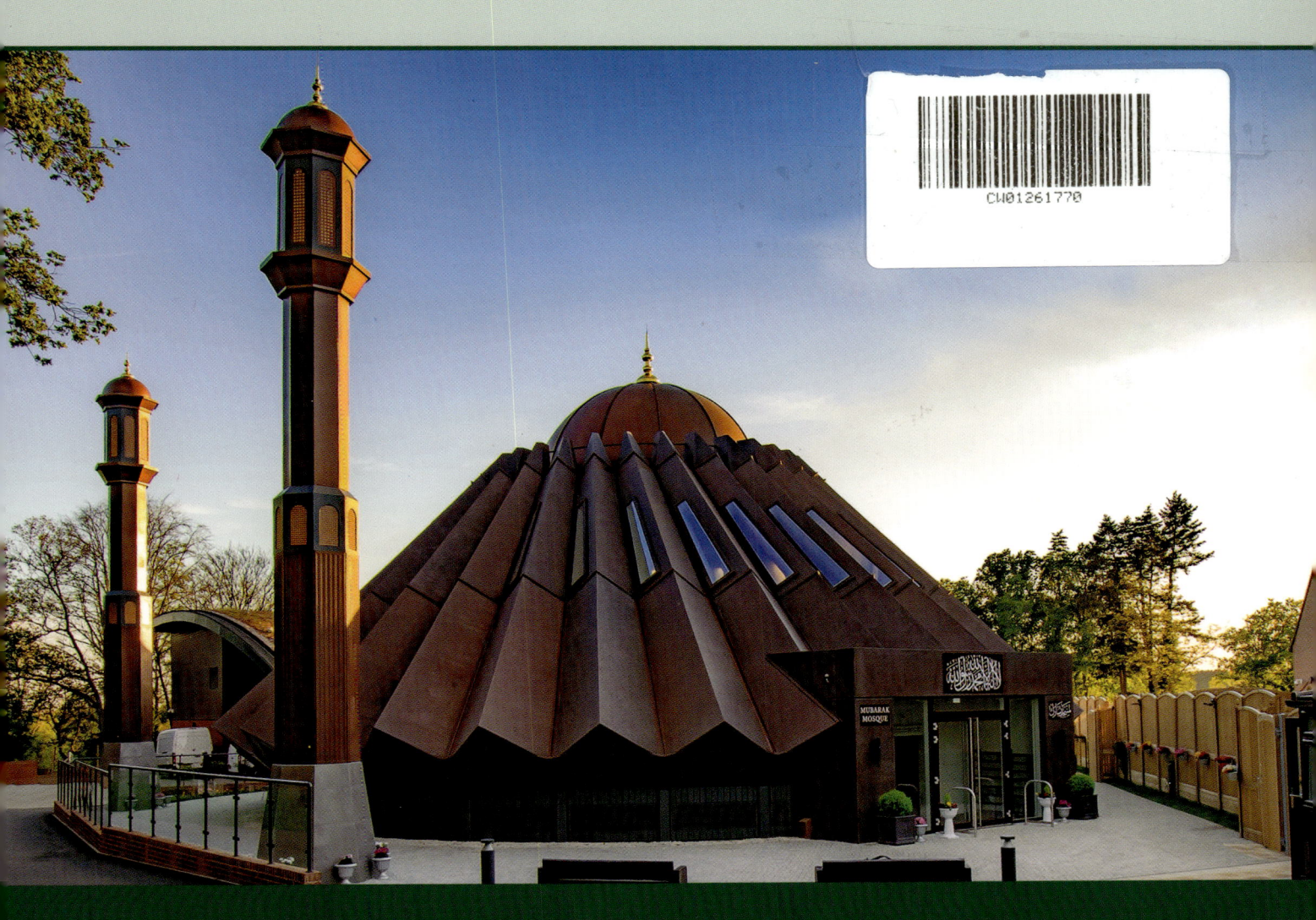

"We strive for interfaith dialogue. We value and cherish our neighbours. We are ever ready to help those who are in need. We champion the rights of the weak and deprived. We are there to serve the community and to be loyal and faithful citizens. This is our faith and this is our teaching."

(His Holiness Hazrat Mirza Masroor Ahmad, Head of the Worldwide Ahmadiyya Muslim Community)

AN BRIEF INTRODUCTION TO THE AHMADIYYA MUSLIM COMMUNITY

The Ahmadiyya Muslim Community is the most dynamic denomination of Islam in modern history, with an estimated membership in the tens of millions spread across 210 countries. In the UK, it is one of the most established Muslim communities and now has 136 branches nationwide.

It was established in 1889 by Hazrat Mirza Ghulam Ahmad (peace be upon him) (1835-1908) *(photo right)* in a small and remote village called Qadian in the Punjab, India. As prophesied by the Holy Prophet Muhammad – (peace and blessings of Allah be upon him), Hazrat Mirza Ghulam Ahmad (peace be upon him) claimed to be the expected reformer of the latter days awaited by all world religions. The community he started is an embodiment of the benevolent message of Islam in its pristine purity that promotes peace and universal brotherhood based on a belief in the Gracious and Ever-Merciful God.

With this conviction, within 130 years, the Ahmadiyya Muslim Community has expanded globally and it serves mankind by raising millions of pounds every year for charities, building schools and hospitals open to all, providing energy to remote villages, encouraging learning through interfaith dialogue and by providing food and water to those in need across the world. The UK chapter of the community was established in 1913.

THE KHALIFA OF ISLAM – A MAN OF PEACE

His Holiness, Hazrat Mirza Masroor Ahmad (may Allah be his Helper) was elected as the fifth Khalifa (Caliph) of the worldwide Ahmadiyya Muslim Community in 2003.

His Holiness inspires the Community to serve humanity with the spirit of kindness and humility that is integral to Islam. In accordance with the teachings of Islam, he upholds the honour of all prophets of God and highlights the role of religion in the promotion of peace.

His Holiness has delivered addresses at the House of Commons, Capitol Hill, the Canadian Parliament and the European Parliament and also written to world leaders urging them to inculcate absolute justice and peace in international relations, to avoid regional conflicts from engulfing the entire world.

In 1924 the Ahmadiyya Muslim Community UK built London's first purpose built mosque – The Fazl Mosque in Southfields, London *(pictured right)*. In 2018, the mosque became a Grade II listed building in recognition of its historical significance to the UK.

The Ahmadiyya Muslim Community built in 2003 the Baitul Futuh Mosque in Morden, Surrey *(pictured top right)*. It is Western Europe's largest mosque and was listed by the *Independent* newspaper magazine as one of the top 50 buildings in the world to visit.

Since its redevelopment was completed in 2019, Islamabad has become the international focus of the worldwide Ahmadiyya Muslim Community.

HISTORICAL

- The site was originally known as Sheephatch School and was initially a wartime evacuation centre in Tilford established in 1939. After the Second World War, it was transformed into a rural centre for problem children of the suburbs of London and later turned into a regular boarding school until it closed down in 1977.

> In 1984, after seeking approval and guidance from the Fourth Khalifa, Hazrat Mirza Tahir Ahmad (may Allah have mercy on him), the land was purchased by the Ahmadiyya Muslim Community and the Khalifa named it 'Islamabad' meaning the 'place where Islam [peace] abides'.
>
> The Fourth Khalifa pictured right at Islamabad performing the first prayer at the site. He passed away in April 2003 and is buried in a special plot in the grounds of Islamabad.

- With the general deteriorating condition of the site, a plan was finalised and with the guidance and approval of His Holiness the Fifth Khalifa of the Ahmadiyya Muslim Community, it was submitted to Waverley Borough Council in 2014. In early 2015, the Council granted building permission for a new mosque and other facilities.

- A central feature of the major refurbishment plan was the new mosque complete with minarets. In addition, a large multi-purpose hall and other residential and administrative buildings were part of the exciting new development.

- There is now also equestrian facilities on-site with a large paddock. These provide equestrian training for the children living on site as well as the children of members living in the UK

- In respect of the residents, there were 33 self-contained residential chalets on site which were in a very poor condition. On the same footprint of the old buildings, 33 new houses were developed.

JALSA SALANA (ANNUAL CONVENTION)

The Islamabad site played host to the Jalsa from 1985 to 2005 where thousands of delegates and special guests including parliamentarians, civic leaders and diplomats from different countries attended a 3-day event to increase religious knowledge and underline the Jalsa's objective of enhancing unity, understanding and mutual respect. The event is now held annualy at the Community's site Hadeeqatul Mahdi which is based in Alton, Hampshire.

AIMS AND VISION OF THE REDEVELOPMENT

- The area of Islamabad is a part of the green belt and all planning and strategy was developed within the confines of maintaining utmost respect and responsibility to honour this status. In addition, the objective was to replace the existing buildings with highly sustainable modern structures which were to be appropriately designed for this context and perform exceptionally in terms of environmental and energy efficient criteria.

- New residential accommodation was formed in the location of the existing terraces, stepped into the falling topography – on the site of the existing residential chalets and overlooking the areas of existing open space within the site. Parking was integrated in small landscaped zones.

- The existing mosque (which was contained within one of the chalets) and sports hall was replaced in a more convenient location shielded from external view by existing tree and landscape cover.

- It was crucial that the site retained its natural residential and operational halves, with all buildings forming a 'campus environment' similar to a small school or university with buildings being constructed using a modern vernacular and clad with timber to help it blend into its woodland context.

- All the properties have been built with solar panels to provide in the main, alternative energy with a grid network also in place when needed. All materials and building works have met with full approval and consultation for the local Council.

- The Ahmadiyya Muslim Community is very grateful for the permission granted to build the mosque, adjoining multi-purpose sports hall and other units. The whole concept has very much been in keeping to energy saving, environment friendly and efficient maintenance through all planning stages. The multi-purpose sports hall itself has a unique green roof with its own ecological system ensuring foliage all year round *(see pic below)*.

The Ahmadiyya Muslim Community is proud of this achievement of transforming the area into a beautiful landmark for the region and taking steps of responsible planning to ensure protection of the environment and developing high standards for ecological placement.

The Mubarak Mosque *(see cover photo)* was inaugurated on Friday 17th May by the unveiling of a plaque by His Holiness, Hazrat Mirza Masroor Ahmad.

During the Friday Sermon, His Holiness emphasised the need for Ahmadi Muslims to present the local residents near Islamabad with the noble teachings of Islam through their pious actions and to pay particular attention to fulfilling the rights of the local residents.

Despite the fact that Islamabad had been established for a long while, His Holiness said now the premises has taken on far greater significance with the construction of the new headquarters and thus Ahmadi Muslims must now be even more concerned than before for the comfort of their neighbours.

His Holiness said:

> "You must now display your best examples even more so than before, and you must leave a good impression on the neighbours. If our neighbours are disturbed due to our noise, or the disorderliness of our traffic, or for any other reason, then we are giving a wrong message to the residents here. In this case, if we are not portraying the correct message of Islam, our gratitude towards Allah the Almighty will be meaningless verbal utterances. Gratitude to Allah the Almighty demands that our words and our actions, our teachings and our deeds should be one and the same, not that we should say one thing and yet act otherwise."

PHOTOS OF THE OLD SITE SHOWING GENERAL LAYOUT AND THE OLD WOODEN STRUCTURES

The late Mr Usman Chou, a retired missionary and one of the first residents in Islamabad since its purchase was appointed by His Holiness (who was on a tour of Canada at the time), to lay the Foundation Stone of the Mubarak Mosque in October 2016.

Sutton Griffin Architects were appointed for the design.

PHOTOS OF ISLAMABAD AFTER REDEVELOPMENT

Interior of the Mubarak Mosque

Arabic calligraphy featured inside the mosque

Part of the Administrative Offices

One of the blocks of residential dwellings

Lushful greenery and plantation adorn the site

Inside the multi-purpose sports hall

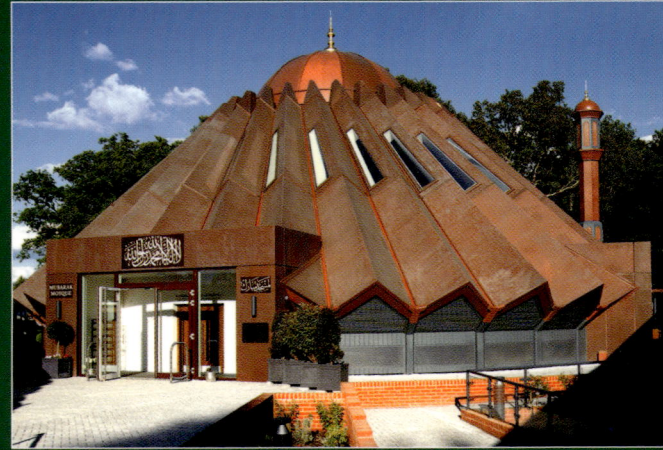

"Pleased to see that this small part of the Surrey countryside is the focus of yet another thriving community dedicated to peaceful living, where we have always been welcome to visit."

(Impressions of the Old Sheeptonians, an alumni association of the school)
Ref: Al-Hakam newsletter

Ahmadiyya Muslim Community UK

Mubarak Mosque, Islamabad

Sheephatch Lane, Tilford, Farnham, GU10 2AQ

www.alislam.org • www.mta.tv • www.LoveForAllHatredForNone.org